This book belongs to

....

ISBN 978-1-64638-591-1

www.cottagedoorpress.com

Cottage Door Press® and the Cottage Door Press® logo
are registered trademarks of Cottage Door Press, LLC.

I Spy with My Little Eye

OUTER SPACE ROAD TRIP

ZOOM & FIND

Written by Rubie Crowe
Illustrated by Steven Wood

cottage door press

Gather around family, let's choose a location — How should we spend our next summer space-cation?

I spy 6 space pens that are blue. Tell me, can you spot them, too?

Some of these brochures are duplicates! Can you spot 4 pamphlets and their matching mates?

WACKY-WATER WORLD

BIGGEST SLIDES IN THE UNIVERSE

MOONSTONE NATURAL PARK

HYPERNOVA CONCERT HALL

GRAND COSMIC CRATER

CHEESEY FAMILY FUN

STAR

Did you remember your toothbrush?

Can you spot a playful cat?

Can you find a flowered hat?

Did you pack enough socks?

Find 2 pairs of sunglasses.

Did you close all the windows
and lock all the locks?

Can you help find
my other shoe?

Let's get the bags loaded
and try to be quick!

I think you forgot
a suitcase!

I spy something that leaves
slimy trails. Can you
count 9 spacey snails?

I spy 7 smiling little shrubs.
Can you spot them, too?

Safety first!
Find the first
aid kit.

These little critters get into everything! Can you find one trying on some headphones?

FIRST AID

If we get going soon, we might just miss the ...

NEXT EXIT
180,000 LIGHT-YEARS AWAY

THE ASTEROID RUN
44

A meteor shower!?
That's the last thing we need!

Could this meteor shower be any meatier? Can you count 7 hot dogs and 4 hamburgers?

Can you find a green meteor?

right everyone, c
ount 4 police ve
ave come to save

I thought meteors were made of stone, but can you spy 2 ice-cream cones?

Can you spot the satellite with the green star?

Something sure seems out of place. Can you find a dog who's lost in space?

And just as we were starting to pick up some speed.

I'll refuel the ship while you go
choose a snack ...

I spy a postcard with a dog in a hat. Look around, can you find that?

ONSTELLATION STATION

Moon Maid is the best drink in town! Can you spot 6 bottles around?

Can you find 4 moon air fresheners?

ON
AID

$350 00

HELLO

LOTTO

$100

WC

Can you spot 2 rocket now-globe souvenirs?

...then use the restroom and hurry right back.

Well, this planet is just as cute as can be.

I spy with my little eye 8 lovely llamas.
Can you find one with sunglasses?
Can you spot one in pajamas?

ICE CREAM

Aww, they're so cute!
Aren't you smitten?
Can you spot
5 purple kittens?

Who's that floating through the crowd?
A raccoon riding on a cloud!
Can you find him?

MOON MAID

MOON MAID

MOON MAID

Can you find a balloon in every color of the rainbow?

Oh, good heavens, one of these is not a lemon!

Complete the pattern. What comes next?

Just one little thing — where exactly are we?

I spy with my little eye some four-legged pants hanging out to dry. Can you spot them, too?

How did we manage to get so turned around?

I see London, I see France, I see someone holding underpants.

Find the hidden color key to decipher a secret message for the family in the planets.

Pardon me, sir, but we've traveled so far —

These little floofs love to explore. Can you count 10? Can you find 1 more?

SHOOTING STAR FALLS

CRATER CITY

SATURN

BLACK HOLE OVERLOOK

NEXT REST STOP 20,000,000 LIGHT-YEARS AWAY

Can you spot a bouncy kangaroo?
Do you think she is lost, too?

I'm just not sure to WHERE.
Could you point out where we are?

This tumbleweed has a twin.
Can you find another
that looks like him?

Are you hungry? You're in luck!
Find the spacey taco truck.

But we need to get way over there.
Can you help figure out how?

We've come such a long way.
Now let's have some fun!